Look Out, Look Out, It's Coming!

by Laura Geringer
pictures by Sue Truesdell

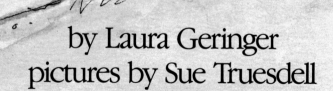

HarperCollinsPublishers

Look Out, Look Out, It's Coming!

by Laura Geringer
pictures by Sue Truesdell

HarperCollins*Publishers*

Look Out, Look Out, It's Coming!
Text copyright © 1992 by Laura Geringer
Illustrations copyright © 1992 by Susan G. Truesdell
Printed in the U.S.A. All rights reserved.
Typography by Al Cetta
1 2 3 4 5 6 7 8 9 10
First Edition

Library of Congress Cataloging-in-Publication Data
Geringer, Laura.
  Look out, look out, it's coming! / by Laura Geringer ; pictures by
Sue Truesdell.
    p.   cm.
  Summary: A huge creature follows a boy home and bounds through his
window during dinner, changing his family's life in drastic and
humorous ways.
  ISBN 0-06-021711-1. — ISBN 0-06-021712-X (lib. bdg.)
  [1. Monsters—Fiction.   2. Stories in rhyme.]   I. Truesdell, Sue,
ill. II. Title.
PZ8.3.G314Lo   1992   91-4707
[E]—dc20   CIP
                                                                  AC

For Ethan
—L.G.

To Pete and Meg
—S.T.

Look Out, Look Out,
It's Coming!

It'll come through your window.

It'll play in your tub.

It'll organize your shadows.

There's nothing it won't rub.

Look out, look out, it's coming!

It'll celebrate a sea storm.

It'll leap and splash and jump.

It'll leave too many footprints.

There's nothing it won't bump.

Look out, look out, it's coming!

It'll ask a thousand questions.

It'll try too hard to guess.

It'll turn nine shades of purple

if you don't say yes.

There's nothing it won't mess.

Look out, look out, it's coming!

It'll blossom in the winter.

It'll grow in the snow.

It'll border on disorder.

There's no place it won't go.

Look out, look out,

it's coming!

Look out, look out...

IT'S COMING!

LAURA GERINGER is the author of A THREE HAT DAY, illustrated by Arnold Lobel, a Reading Rainbow Feature Book and an ALA Notable Children's Book of 1985; MOLLY'S NEW WASHING MACHINE, illustrated by Petra Mathers, a *New York Times* Best Illustrated Book of 1986; THE COW IS MOOING ANYHOW, illustrated by Dirk Zimmer; YOURS 'TIL THE ICE CRACKS, illustrated by Andrea Baruffi; and SILVERPOINT, a novel. Ms. Geringer is a children's book editor at a major publishing house and lives in New York City with her husband and two sons, Adam and Ethan.

A graduate of the Pratt Institute, **SUE TRUESDELL** has illustrated many books for children, including THE GOLLY SISTERS GO WEST and HOORAY FOR THE GOLLY SISTERS! by Betsy Byars; ADDIE MEETS MAX and ADDIE RUNS AWAY by Joan Robins; DONNA O'NEESHUCK WAS CHASED BY SOME COWS by Bill Grossman, an IRA/CBC Children's Choice for 1989; and DABBLE DUCK by Anne Leo Ellis, a Reading Rainbow selection. Ms. Truesdell was chosen to create a streamer for the Children's Book Council's 1992 National Children's Book Week. She lives in New Jersey.